Three Stories about Everyone's Favorite Puppy

Hello, Biscuit! Treasury

by ALYSSA SATIN CAPUCILLI
pictures by PAT SCHORIES

BACKPACKBOOKS

°

NEW YORK

Hello, Biscuit!

Biscuit's Picnic

Happy Birthday, Biscuit!

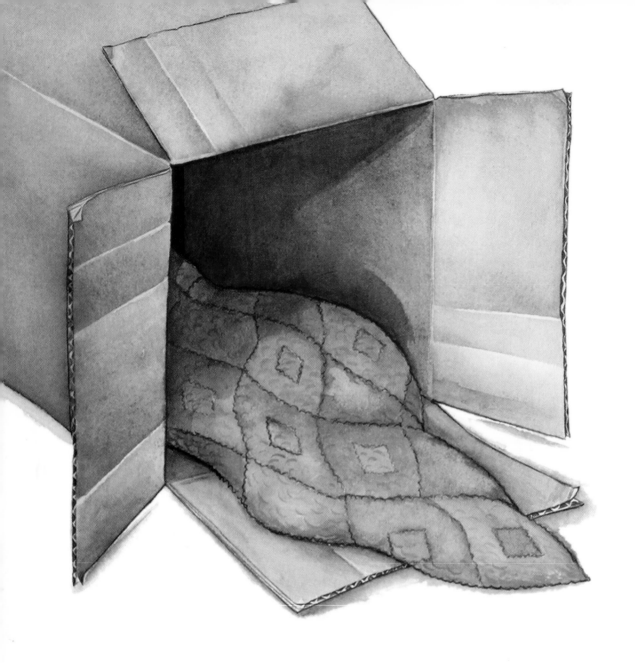

"Here we are, puppy," said the little girl.
"Welcome to your new home!"
      Woof, woof!

"The first thing we must do
is find a name for you.
Let's see. You are small and yellow . . ."
Woof, woof!

"Silly puppy! Come back here!"
 Woof!
"You found your bed,
and your bone,
and your biscuits."
 Woof, woof!

"But no biscuits yet," said the little girl.
"First we must find a name for you!"

"Let's see. You are small and yellow . . .
Wait, little puppy! Where are you going now?"

Woof, woof!
"You found your ball and your toys."
Woof!
"And you found your biscuits again!"
Woof, woof!

"See?" said the little girl.
"You have everything a puppy could need.
Everything except a name!"
Woof, woof!

"Now, what is your name going to be?"
    Woof!
"Silly puppy! How did you get those biscuits?"
    Woof, woof!

"Oh no! Come back here with those biscuits!"
Woof, woof, woof, woof!

"That's it!" the little girl cried. "Biscuit!"
     Woof!
"Biscuit is the perfect name for you!"
     Woof, woof!

"Hello, Biscuit!
You found a name all by yourself!"

Woof!

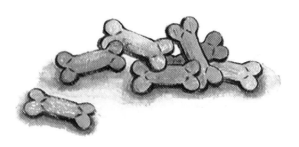

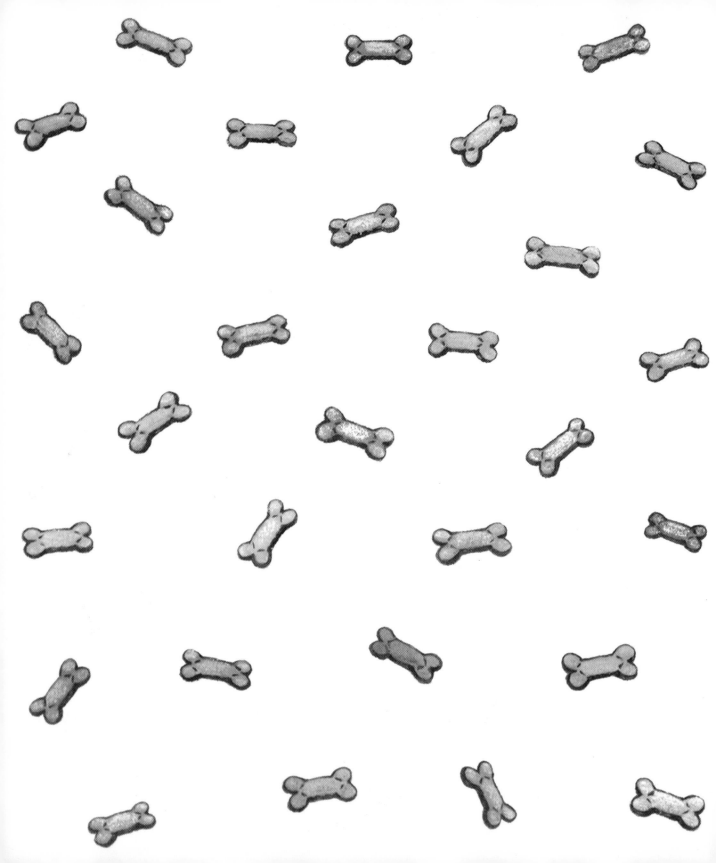

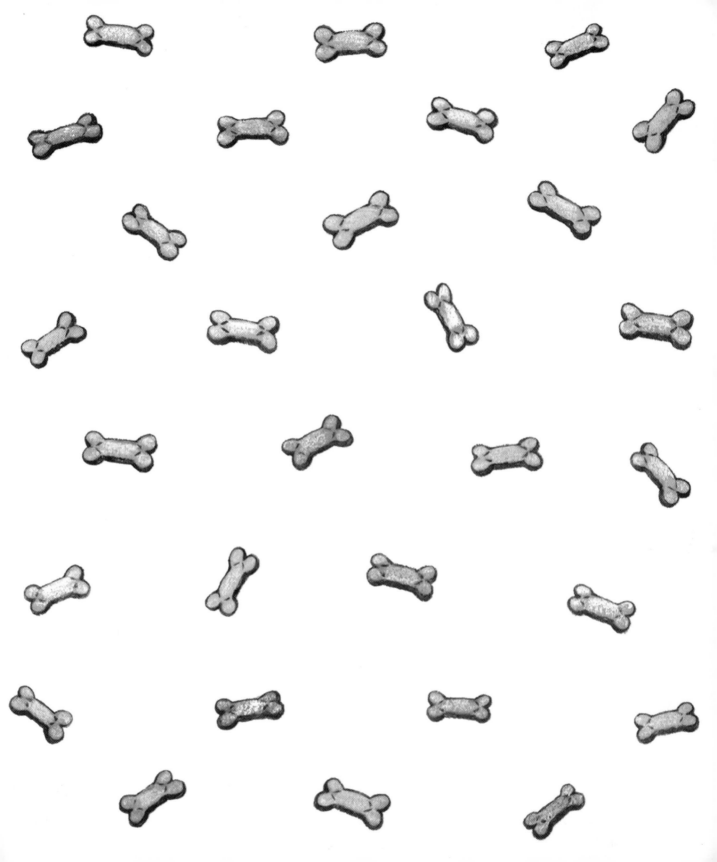

Biscuit
wants to join the picnic,
but he is not invited.
What will he do?

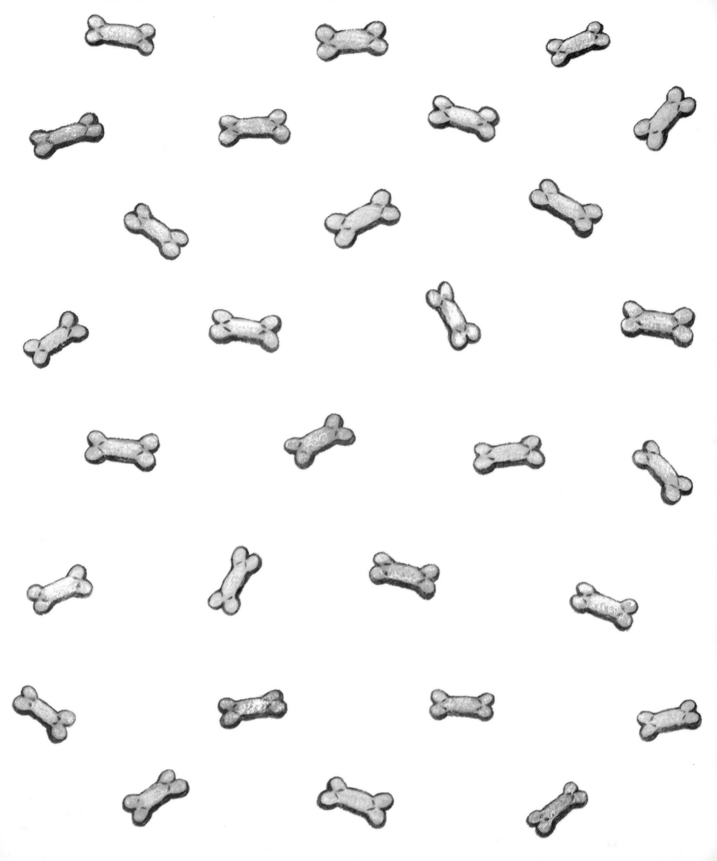

Biscuit's Picnic

"Biscuit, where are you?"
called the little girl.

Woof, woof!

"Silly puppy! What are you doing under there?"

Woof!

"I'm sorry, Biscuit. This picnic is just for kids.
You and Puddles can run and play."

Bow wow!
Woof, woof!
"Go on, puppies. Go and play!"

"Wait, Biscuit! Come back, Puddles!
Where are you going with that food?"

Tweet, tweet, tweet.

"Look!" The little girl laughed.
"Biscuit and Puddles are having
their own picnic—

and the birds want
to join them."

Bow wow!
Woof, woof, woof!

Meow.

"Even Daisy wants to have a picnic!"

Meow.

Woof, woof!

Bow wow, bow wow!

"Careful, Biscuit!" said the little girl.
"Watch out for the—

—CAKE!"

"Biscuit is covered in cake!"
the little boy giggled.
"Oh, Biscuit," said the little girl.
"What do we do now?"

Woof, woof!

"Funny puppy. You're right, Biscuit," she said.
"We can all have a picnic together!"
Woof!

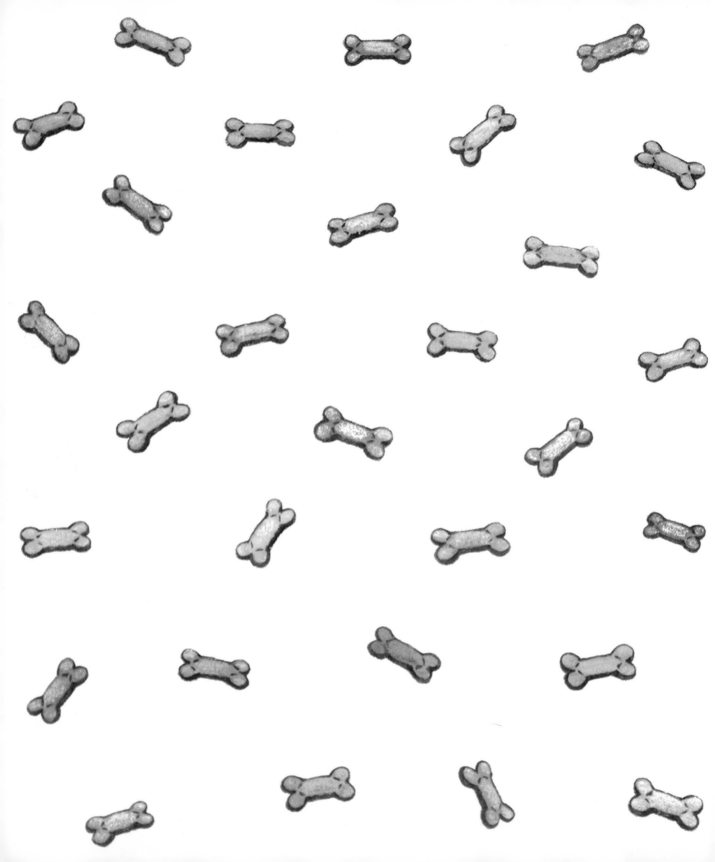

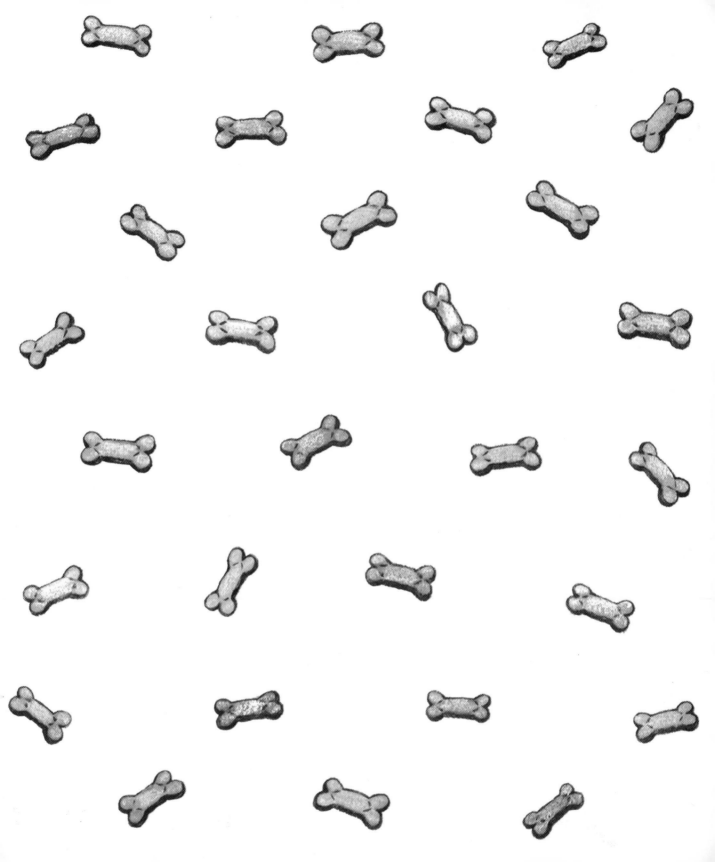

Come celebrate Biscuit's birthday!

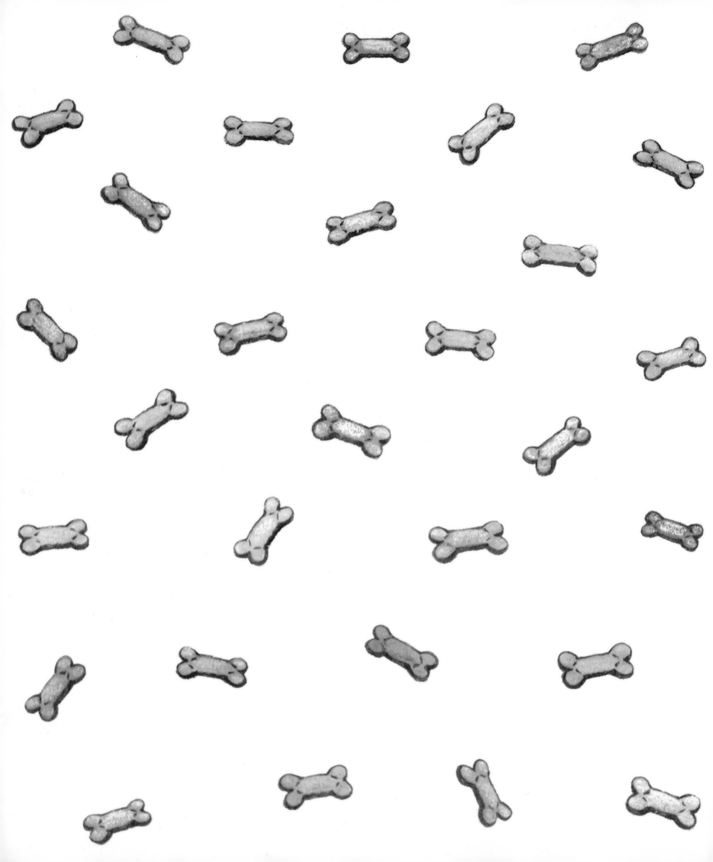

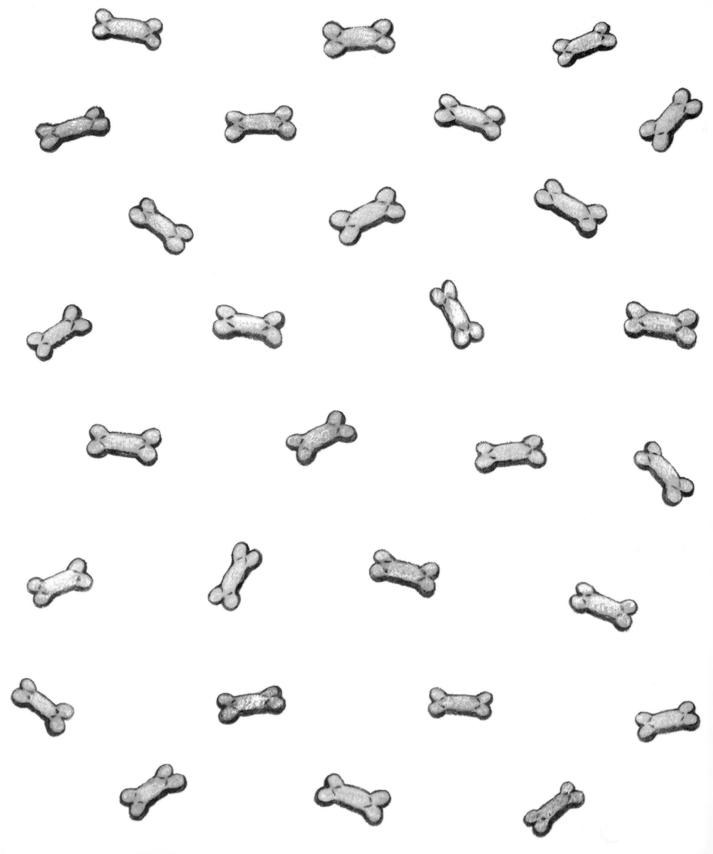

Happy Birthday, Biscuit!

"Wake up, sleepy Biscuit!" said the little girl.
"Do you know what day it is?"

Woof!

"Today is a very special day. It's your birthday!"
Woof! Woof!

"Follow me, Biscuit," said the little girl.
"I have something special planned just for you."

"Surprise, Biscuit! Puddles and Daisy
are here for your birthday party!"

Bow wow!
Meow!

"Come along, everybody.
It's time to play some birthday games."

Woof, woof!
Meow!
Bow wow!

"Silly Biscuit!" called the little girl.
"Be careful with those balloons."

"Oh no," said the little girl. "There go the balloons!"
Woof!

"Oh, Biscuit!" laughed the little girl. "You may be a year older, but you will always be my silly little puppy."

"Now it's time for birthday treats," said the little girl. "Make a wish, Biscuit."

Woof!

"Funny puppy! You want to open your birthday presents!"

"Look, Biscuit! A new collar, a new bone, and best of all . . ."

Woof, woof!

"A new box of biscuits!
Happy Birthday, Biscuit!"
Woof!

Hello, Biscuit!
Biscuit's Picnic
Happy Birthday, Biscuit!

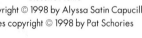

A BACKPACK BOOKS edition, published by permission of
HarperCollins Children's Books
Hello, Biscuit! Treasury
Text copyright © 2002 by Alyssa Satin Capucilli
Pictures copyright © 2002 by Pat Schories

Hello, Biscuit!
Text copyright © 1998 by Alyssa Satin Capucilli
Pictures copyright © 1998 by Pat Schories

Biscuit's Picnic
Text copyright © 1998 by Alyssa Satin Capucilli
Pictures copyright © 1998 by Pat Schories

Happy Birthday, Biscuit!
Text copyright © 1999 by Alyssa Satin Capucilli
Pictures copyright © 1999 by Pat Schories

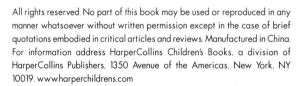